DRAGONBREATH

WHEN FAIRIES GO BAD

DRAGONBREATH
WHEN FAIRIES GO BAD

BY
URSULA VERNON

DIAL BOOKS

an imprint of Penguin Group (USA) Inc.

*This one's for all the coffee shops in Pittsboro, North Carolina,
where the great majority of the Dragonbreath books have been written.
Without bottomless cups of coffee and extra cream, Danny would be
much less zany.*

DIAL BOOKS
An imprint of Penguin Group (USA) Inc.
Published by The Penguin Group • Penguin Group (USA) Inc., 375 Hudson Street, New York, NY 10014,
U.S.A. • Penguin Group (Canada), 90 Eglinton Avenue East, Suite 700, Toronto, Ontario, Canada M4P 2Y3
(a division of Pearson Penguin Canada Inc.) • Penguin Books Ltd, 80 Strand, London WC2R 0RL, England •
Penguin Ireland, 25 St. Stephen's Green, Dublin 2, Ireland (a division of Penguin Books Ltd) • Penguin Group
(Australia), 250 Camberwell Road, Camberwell, Victoria 3124, Australia (a division of Pearson Australia
Group Pty Ltd) • Penguin Books India Pvt Ltd, 11 Community Centre, Panchsheel Park, New Delhi - 110 017,
India • Penguin Group (NZ), 67 Apollo Drive, Rosedale, Auckland 0632, New Zealand (a division of Pearson
New Zealand Ltd) • Penguin Books (South Africa) (Pty) Ltd, 24 Sturdee Avenue, Rosebank, Johannesburg
2196, South Africa • Penguin Books Ltd, Registered Offices: 80 Strand, London WC2R 0RL, England

Designed by Jennifer Kelly
Text set in Stempel Schneidler
Printed in the U.S.A.

10 9 8 7 6 5 4 3 2 1

Library of Congress Cataloging-in-Publication Data
Vernon, Ursula.
   When fairies go bad / by Ursula Vernon.   p. cm. — (Dragonbreath ; 7)
Summary: Danny's mother has disappeared into a fairy ring growing in her backyard vegetable garden,
and Danny and his friends Wendell and Christiana must go to Faerie to try to save her.
ISBN 978-0-8037-3678-8 (hardcover)
[1. Adventure and adventurers—Fiction. 2. Fairies—Fiction. 3. Dragons—Fiction. 4. Iguanas—Fiction.
5. Humorous stories.] I. Title.
PZ7.V5985Whe 2012
[Fic]—dc23   2011048053

IT WON EVERY PRIZE AT THE FAIR, INCLUDING A FEW IT WASN'T TECHNICALLY ELIGIBLE FOR. THERE WAS TALK OF THE GUINNESS BOOK OF WORLD RECORDS.

IT WAS THE FIRST FRUIT VISIBLE FROM SPACE.

MUSHROOM INVASION

"Danny," his mother said, and then somewhat louder, *"Danny!"*

"Huh? What?" Danny looked up, startled.

"I think you've watered it enough." His mother studied the brown puddle that surrounded the tiny pumpkin seedling. "More than enough, really . . ."

"Oh!" Danny hastily pulled the hose away. His plant looked like a tiny green island in a sea of soggy dirt. "Did I hurt it? Is it okay?"

"It'll be fine. Plants are tougher than they look."

Danny squelched happily through the damp garden soil to hang the hose back up. He liked gardening. Well, he liked *some* gardening. The exciting bits anyway, like when you got to use shovels and trowels and other implements of destruction to dig holes and trenches and make mounds of earth.

Harvesting was okay, for the first ten minutes, since there was something at least semi-destructive about wrenching stuff off stems, except that then you had to eat it for dinner and it was all vegetables, sort of by definition. The raw peas were pretty good, when you could crack the pod with your thumb and eat them right there, but you were still dealing with vegetables, and a bad candy bar tended to beat a good vegetable any day of the week.

He wasn't fond of weeding either. It always seemed to involve putting his hand on a slug. Neither he nor the slug enjoyed this. It was gross, and not in a fun way, just in a squishy way.

Ever since his mom had gotten into organic gardening and had turned the backyard into a vegetable garden, there was plenty of weeding to go around and more vegetables than any sane kid could be expected to eat.

Some of them were *weird* vegetables too.

HONEY?
WHAT AM I
SUPPOSED TO DO
WITH ALL THESE
RUTABAGAS?

Danny sighed. Still, he'd get to grow his own pumpkin. The seed packet had a photo of a pumpkin bigger than the farmer who grew it. How cool was *that*?

He wished Wendell the iguana were here. Then if he got slug slime on his hands, he could at least chase Wendell around with it.

Probably sensing that the natives were growing restless, Danny's mother looked up from her tray of seedlings. "I don't think I need any more help today, Danny," she said, which was parent-speak for "Go find something else to do."

"Okay!" Danny sprinted for the patio.

He got about halfway there, caught his foot on something, and sprawled face-first into the grass.

"Danny!" His mother jumped up. "Are you okay?"

Danny sat up, scrubbing at his scales with his sleeve. "Yeah, I'm fine . . . I think. Something tripped me!"

"Tripped you?"

The two dragons peered down at the culprit.

"That's a big mushroom," said Danny. It was nearly as large as his head.

"I'm surprised I didn't notice it earlier," said his mother. "And surprised you didn't smash it when you fell—that must be one tough mushroom!"

Danny reached out to poke it, and his mother grabbed his hand. "Don't! Big spotted mushrooms like that are usually poisonous!" She frowned down at the mushroom.

"There's another one over there," said Danny, pointing. "And I think I see one over there too . . ."

A WHAT?

"That's what people used to call mushroom rings. They said the fairies would come and dance in them."

Danny wrinkled his snout. "Fairies? You mean the little thingies with the wings on girls' lunch boxes?"

His mom laughed. "Don't make that face—I had fairies on *my* lunch box too, when I was a girl. But I don't think they really look like that, if they even exist at all."

"You mean they aren't real?" Danny considered this. "Like *really* not real, or like mythical-not-real?" Being a dragon himself, he was used to mythical creatures. Some of the people who showed up at family reunions were unusual, to say the least.

"I don't really know," his mom admitted.

"Nobody in the family has ever seen one, I don't think, although your great-grandfather claims they get in at night and steal the spoons."

Danny had no problem believing this. Great-Grandfather Dragonbreath was notably eccentric, even in a family that included Danny, and that was saying something.

"Anyway," his mother said, "some mushrooms just grow in rings, no fairies required. I'd better go on the Internet and find out what kind it is. If it's poisonous and one springs up in the vegetable beds . . ." She reached out with her gardening gloves and grabbed the malicious mushroom by the stalk. It cracked off at the base, revealing squishy white flesh.

Wrinkling her nose, his mother headed toward the house. Danny cast a last look over his shoulder at the other mushrooms, then followed.

THE MOM-NAPPING

Danny woke up in the night and knew that something strange was going on.

He could hear music.

His dad sometimes got insomnia and listened to the radio late at night—usually country, which was all about heartbreak and misery and women who done you wrong. (Danny hated country music.) But Danny's father was out of town for the week on business, and anyway, this wasn't country. This music was all swirly and skirling and full of pipes. There were no words . . . about women who done you wrong or otherwise.

It was kind of interesting, actually.

Without quite realizing it, Danny had gotten out of bed. He went to the window and looked down into the backyard. The music seemed louder, and he could hear drums now.

If he opened the window, he might be able to climb down—he was getting too big for the rain gutter to really support his weight, and he'd decided not to do that anymore after the last time, when he'd nearly torn it off the side of the house—but there was something about that music. He wanted to see where it was coming from.

The back door banged. Danny jumped.

His mother walked into the backyard. She was wearing a bathrobe, and she was looking around, as if trying to locate the music herself.

You should come down, the music said, without words. *Come closer.*

Don't be stupid, said Danny's brain, *your mom is standing right there, and if she sees you coming down the rain gutter, you are gonna get in so much trouble—!*

Come down, whispered the music. *Come closer, foolish woman who pulled our mushrooms . . .*

His mom walked forward, into the grass. Danny realized two things, more or less simultaneously—first of all, the music wasn't talking to *him,* and secondly, the mushroom ring was *glowing.*

Danny might not be as smart as his friends Wendell and Christiana, but he'd read enough comic books to know that you didn't mess around with strange stuff that glowed.

This was a bad glow too. It was greenish gray and it flickered and throbbed. It looked unhealthy, like it would give you some horrible disease if you touched it.

"Mom!" Danny yelled out the window.

His mother stopped at the edge of the fairy ring and looked around vaguely. "Danny?" he heard her say. "Danny, do you hear—"

It was too late. As she turned toward him, her arm passed over the line of mushrooms.

The music rose to a screaming whine, and *something* reached out of the fairy ring, closed over Danny's mother's wrist, and yanked her into the ring.

She vanished. The music halted as if it had been cut with a knife.

MOM!

The glow of the mushrooms began to fade. By the time Danny had catapulted across his bed, pounded down the hallway, hurtled the stairs, and skidded through the kitchen to reach the backyard, it was nearly gone. A few sickly green flashes clung to the mushroom gills, and then faded.

Danny groped for the light switch and turned on the patio light. He could see the dark trail of footsteps that his mother had left in the wet grass, leading up to the fairy ring, but that was all.

His mom was gone.

Something in the fairy ring had taken her.

A REAL NIGHTMARE

Danny woke up feeling enormously relieved. He'd had an awful nightmare, a real brain-burner, but he was awake now. Although he was really cold, come to think of it, and his neck hurt, and was he *wet*?

He had a brief, horrifying notion that he might have wet the bed. There were probably more humiliating things that could happen to a dragon, but he couldn't think of any.

He sat up in a hurry and realized that for some reason he had been asleep in one of the deck chairs on the patio.

He was soaked because the dew had settled on him. But why would he be sleeping on the patio?

Unless . . .

Danny slowly turned, ignoring the pain in his neck, and saw the mushroom ring.

The mushrooms weren't glowing anymore, but the trail of footprints was still dimly visible through the silver grass.

It wasn't a dream...

He bolted into the house, yelling, "MOM! Mom, where are you?"

There was no answer. The kitchen was cold. The coffeepot had turned on automatically, but the pot was full and hadn't been touched, which was conclusive proof that Danny's mother was nowhere on this mortal plane. Mrs. Dragonbreath went nowhere without coffee.

Danny gulped. There was only one explanation, then. His dream had been real, and that meant—

"You're telling me that *fairies* took your mother?" said Wendell.

The iguana wasn't entirely pleased at being on the phone—normally on Saturday mornings he was watching cartoons and trying to choke down his mother's bran waffles. Danny was interrupting *Skate Force,* just as the villain was about to feed Landshark into a giant laser.

"I'm serious!" said Danny. "She's *gone!*"

"Have you called the police?" asked Wendell, stabbing another bit of waffle. Low-calorie organic sodium-free agave nectar syrup-alternative was congealing around the edges. The bran waffles had the dubious distinction of weighing more than the waffle iron they were cooked on, and they sat in your stomach like a syrup-coated bowling ball.

"What am I going to tell the police?" snapped Danny. "I saw my mom go into a mushroom ring last night and now she's gone? They'll never believe me! They didn't believe me last month about the body snatchers!"

IN FAIRNESS, THE BODY SNATCHERS WERE CLEVERLY DISGUISED AS GIRL SCOUTS.

SELLING COOKIES.

THEY SHOULD HAVE AT LEAST SENT A SQUAD CAR TO CHECK IT OUT!

Wendell rubbed his forehead. "What does your dad say?"

"He's out of town." Danny leaned against the refrigerator. "He won't be back until Monday night. And I tried to call him, but his phone's not charged. He never remembers to charge his phone. Mom's always yelling at him about it."

Wendell heaved a sigh. "Maybe she just went to the grocery store early or something."

Danny played his trump card. "The coffeepot hasn't been touched."

There was a long silence on the other end of the phone. Then the tinny sounds of *Skate Force* switched off and a distant thud, as of a bran waffle being dropped into the trash.

"Right," said Wendell. "This is an *emergency*. I'll be there in twenty minutes."

THE DRAGONBREATH WAY

"I've called Christiana," Wendell announced. "She'll be here as soon as she can."

"You've got her phone number?" asked Danny. "What's up with *that*?"

"What?" Wendell shoved his glasses up his snout. "We're lab partners. We talk on the phone every time we've got an assignment."

Danny wasn't sure if he believed that, but then again, Wendell and Christiana were in the super-advanced science class, and Danny was in the class where the teacher watched him like a hawk and jumped on him if he so much as looked at the hydrochloric acid. Danny was pretty sure that Wendell could walk out of the school with a gallon of acid under each arm. Life was so unfair.

Anyway, this was not the time to tease Wendell about maybe having a girlfriend.

I DIDN'T TELL HER THE REASON. YOU CAN EXPLAIN THAT YOURSELF.

DUDE, SHE'S NOT GOING TO BELIEVE ME ABOU᠎ THE FAIRIES.

I'M NOT SURE IF *I* BELIEVE YOU ABOUT THE FAIRIES.

"I'm telling you, I saw my mom walk into the mushroom ring! Come look! And there was this weird music and everything!"

Wendell plodded into the backyard after him to see the mushrooms. "Hmm. Well, they're mushrooms, all right. They look kinda poisonous."

"That's what Mom said."

FAIRIES.

UH-HUH.

LIKE THE THINGS HALF OUR CLASS DRESSED UP AS FOR HALLOWEEN BACK IN THIRD GRADE.

"Yeah."

Wendell stepped back. "Is this the bit where you tell me that dragons know all about fairies and your great-grandmother was a fairy?"

"Unfortunately, no." Danny frowned down at the mushrooms. "Mom didn't know if they were real or not. I've never met one. The only thing I've heard . . ."

He stopped, because it was too dumb even to tell Wendell.

"Yes?"

Danny took a deep breath. "My great-grandfather thinks they get in at night and steal the spoons." It sounded even worse when he said it out loud.

"Oh no," said Wendell. "I am *not* going to see your great-grandfather again. He always calls me Wanda."

"I dunno, you kinda look like a Wanda . . ." said Christiana, opening the gate in the fence and letting herself into the backyard. The crested lizard tromped across the grass, exchanged a friendly elbow-in-the-ribs with Wendell, and turned to Danny. "Wendell said it was urgent. What's up?"

Danny sighed. It seemed unfair that he had

to deal with Junior Skeptic Christiana on top of having his mom disappear. On the other hand, Christiana was the only person he knew who was as smart as Wendell, and he needed all the help he could get.

SO I WOKE UP IN THE MIDDLE OF THE NIGHT, AND THERE WAS THIS WEIRD MUSIC . . .

Being a lizard, Christiana didn't blink very much to begin with, but there was a quality to that unwinking stare that made Danny uncomfortable. You got the impression that she thought you were making the world a stupider place merely by talking into it.

"So then I called Wendell," he finished. "And . . . uh . . . yeah."

"Did you call the police?" asked Christiana. Wendell grinned, then tried to hide it behind a hand.

"They won't believe me," said Danny tiredly. "*You* don't believe me, and you saw the ghost last year, and the jackalope and everything."

"The possible existence of ghosts—which we have not been able to replicate—does not prove anything about the existence of fairies," said Christiana. "And the jackalope was a straightforward example of applied cryptozoology. An exciting discovery, but it doesn't prove that any other cryptid necessarily exists."

"Look," said Danny, feeling discouraged, "whatever you just said is probably true in nerd-speak, but the fact is, my mom's GONE, and I saw her walk into that—*Wendell, no!*"

Wendell had been poking one of the mushrooms with a stick. He was so surprised that Danny was yelling at him to stop doing something—generally it was the other way around—that he fell over, directly into the fairy ring.

Danny had expected something slightly awful to happen when Wendell fell into the ring—a puff of smoke, more music, Wendell disappearing or possibly exploding—but nothing happened. The mushrooms just sat there, looking sinister. Wendell looked confused.

"I thought something would happen," said Danny. "I kinda hoped . . . I mean, I thought if nothing else, we'd be able to follow her." This was very depressing. If the mushroom ring didn't work, how would he go after his mom? How would he get her back?

What was his dad going to say?

"Maybe it only works at night," said Wendell, patting his shoulder.

"Maybe they're just mushrooms and you dreamed the whole thing," said Christiana. She crouched down and examined the nearest mushroom. "Looks like an *Amanita* to me. They're really poisonous. Some of them make you hallucinate too."

COULD DANNY HAVE HAD A HALLUCINATION?

SINCE HE'D HAVE DIED RIGHT AFTER, PROBABLY NOT. YOU'RE NOT ABOUT TO DIE, ARE YOU?

NO, I THINK I'M OKAY... EXCEPT FOR THE BIT WHERE MY MOM IS *MISSING!*

Wendell stood up. "Look," he said, "let's assume for the sake of argument that maybe fairies exist and they did take Danny's mother. I've seen some pretty weird things. What would we do next?"

Christiana frowned. "Try to learn more about them, I suppose. Do we know any experts?"

"There's Danny's great-grandfather," said Wendell. "But I'm *not* going back to mythical Japan to talk to him. No way, no how. There were ninjas. And he called me Wanda."

"We don't have to," said Danny. "My mom bought him a phone after our last visit. The number's on the fridge."

"Then we should consult with our expert," said Christiana. She rolled her eyes a little. "But I still think we should call the police . . ."

"If Great-Granddad doesn't know anything, we will," promised Danny. "But first we're gonna try it the Dragonbreath way."

SECRET OF THE SPOONS

Great-Grandfather Dragonbreath grew deafer with each passing year, so it took about twenty rings before he picked up the phone. When he finally did, he said "Eh? What?" instead of hello.

Danny was used to all that. "Great-Granddad! It's Danny! It's an emergency!"

"Danny, is it? Speak up, boy, don't mumble." His great-grandfather punched a few buttons, trying to find the one that turned the volume up. Danny winced at the loud beeping in his ear, but waited for the old dragon to finish.

"Danny . . . Danny . . . right, right. How's your little reincarnated friend?"

"I think Suki's fine, Great-Granddad! That's not why I'm calling!"

"And Wanda, how's Wanda?"

"Wendell's fine, Great-Granddad. This is important! Listen up! Fairies kidnapped my mom!"

"Fairies—!" There was a crash as Great-Grandfather Dragonbreath dropped the phone. He picked it up again. "Should've known they wouldn't stick to spoons," he muttered. "Nasty thieving brutes."

"There's got to be a way!" said Danny.

"Of course there's a way," said Great-Grandfather Dragonbreath. "You're brave and not very bright, which is the key to success, and you've got little Wanda with you. I'm confident you can get her back."

Danny felt a wave of relief crash over him. He let out a breath that felt like it came from the bottom of his toes.

"The odds of you dying a painful, horrible death are hardly worth mentioning!" his great-grandfather said cheerfully. "I assume you can find a way into the fairy realm yourself, Danny? You got into mythical Japan just fine . . ."

"I'll check the bus schedule," Danny promised.

"Good, good. Now, there are a few rules to keep in mind once you're there. First off, don't eat *anything* you don't bring yourself, or you'll be trapped there forever. And don't tell anyone your real name. Names have power over there. You'll find a path. Don't stray off it, no matter how tempted you are. If you're on the path, you'll be protected. Once you step off . . . well, things could get messy. And once you've found her . . ." There was a clicking noise as the old dragon drummed his claws on the handset of the phone. "Put Wanda on the phone, will you?"

IT'S *WENDELL,*
MR. DRAGONBREATH . . .

Christiana snickered. So did Danny.

"Uh-huh," said Wendell. "No, *Wendell,* not—oh, never mind. Uh-huh . . . no food, got it . . . uh-huh . . . uh-huh . . . let me get a pen." He pulled the notepad off the counter and began writing quickly. Danny peered over his shoulder, and read *Relinquish her of your own free will, and vow by ash and oak and rowan tree not to pursue nor harry us, nor cause a hand to be raised against us in our swift departure from this realm.*

"Uh-huh," said Wendell again, and then held up the pad and read the words off.

Apparently they met with Great-Grandfather Dragonbreath's approval. Wendell listened for another minute, then said, "Yes, sir," and handed the phone back to Danny.

"Told Wanda the words," said Great-Grandfather Dragonbreath. "When you find her, you'll probably have to win her back or trade something for her. At that point, read those words to whoever's holding her, and don't change anything. Those words'll bind them. Otherwise they'll be chasing you the whole way back, and fairies are mean little cusses. Forget anything you think you know about 'em. They aren't sweet, they don't grant wishes, and they'll as soon turn you into a frog as look at you."

"That doesn't sound so bad . . ." said Danny cautiously.

"The non-talking kind of frog! The animal kind!"

EEP.

"Anyway, my show's on," said Great-Grandfather Dragonbreath. "Give a call if you get your mom back. She's my favorite granddaughter, you know . . ."

Danny privately felt that this would have been a more touching tribute if his great-grandfather could remember any of his grandkids' names from one day to the next, but promised to do so and hung up. He looked over to where Christiana and Wendell were conferring.

"This is ridiculous," said Christiana, rolling her eyes, "but if you want to make a fool of yourselves, far be it from me not to come along and watch."

"This way you'll get to say *I told you so,*" said Wendell agreeably. Danny had a sneaking suspicion that Wendell was looking forward to finally proving something to the Junior Skeptic once and for all. The iguana pushed his glasses up on his snout again. "We'll need food, I guess. And probably some other supplies." He waved the sheet of paper with the ritual words on them. "I'll hold on to these."

"Did he tell you anything else?" Danny asked.

"He said we should bring something to bargain with," said Wendell. The iguana frowned. "Although I'm not sure what fairies would want . . ."

"I only know one thing," said Danny, yanking open the silverware drawer. "And we'll make sure we have plenty."

"You've lost your minds," said Christiana.

BACK ON THE BUS

"A bus to fairyland," said Christiana. "*Now* I've seen everything."

"Properly, it's called *Faerie*," said Wendell, looking up from his book. "And they don't like to be called fairies. They're 'the fair folk' or 'the good neighbors.'"

"I question the reliability of your source," muttered Christiana, slouching down on the bus seat.

Wendell held his book protectively to his chest. "It's as good as anything. I brought it because you never know what'll come in handy . . ."

"It's a book of fairy tales," said the crested lizard scornfully.

"Hey! I loved this book when I was little." The iguana stroked the cover affectionately. "My grandmother got this for me. Mom didn't want me to read it because she said it was politically incorrect and would give me nightmares."

DID IT?

OH, A COUPLE. BUT THEY WERE AWESOME STORIES!

FAIRY TALES OFTEN REFLECT A WEALTH OF VALUABLE PSYCHOLOGICAL INSIGHTS ABOUT THE CULTURES THAT CREATED THEM.

...

WHAT?

Fortunately for Danny's sanity, the bus reached their stop. They got out and waited.

"This doesn't look like Faerie . . ." said Christiana. She sounded a bit puzzled. "I'm not actually sure where we are, though. I didn't realize we'd reached such a rural area . . ."

The road was made of a dull gold brick, and led through distant cornfields. Several hundred yards away, an enormous field of poppies reared their scarlet heads in the sun.

"This isn't our final stop," said Danny. "We just need to transfer here."

Wendell, who was used to the way that the city bus system reached some very unusual destinations when Danny was involved, sat down to wait.

Far off in the distance, a house appeared high in the sky and fell to the ground. Christiana's jaw dropped.

"I wouldn't worry about it," said a passing flying monkey, perching briefly on top of the bus sign. "It happens a lot around here." It launched itself off the sign and flapped lazily away.

"Did you see that?!" yelled Christiana, staring after the monkey. "Great Newton's ghost! It talked! And it had four legs *and* wings!"

"The bus is here," said Danny, hiking up his backpack.

"But—"

"We can talk about it on the bus," said Wendell. Danny noticed that the iguana was grinning broadly, and he couldn't blame him.

For the entire ride, Christiana did not shut up about the flying monkey.

"A talking mammal!" she said, for about the hundredth time. "It's unheard of! It must have been some kind of bat, like a flying fox, but the front legs—there simply *aren't* any six-legged vertebrates—I wonder if the bones in the hand or forearm could have split to provide a vestigial hand . . . ?"

"Like a panda's thumb," said Wendell absently, gazing out the window.

"What about panda thumbs?" It was one of

those buses that had a line of seats facing each other up front, and Danny was amusing himself by standing up and holding on to the metal pole, pretending to surf.

WHAT'S SO SPECIAL ABOUT PANDA THUMBS?

"They look like they've got six fingers," said Wendell. "But they don't. Their thumb's actually a bone in their wrist that got all mutated."

"Cool!" Danny swung around the pole, earning a grim look from the bus driver.

"They aren't very good thumbs, though," said Wendell. "You wouldn't want to make a hand that way. It'd be a lousy hand."

"We didn't get a good look at its hands," said

Christiana defensively. "And anyway, that's just a theory. We need to convince a monkey to come back with us and take X-rays to be sure."

Danny didn't see what the big deal was about talking mammals. He'd talked with rats, and his cousin Spencer could talk to jackalopes . . . well, sort of talk. It wasn't exactly words, but they could communicate, anyway, so obviously there were some pretty smart mammals out there.

On the other hand, raving about the monkey was keeping Christiana from making cutting remarks about fairies, and that was fine by Danny.

CAMERA. I HAVE GOT TO GET A CAMERA AND GO BACK. NO, PEOPLE WOULD THINK THE PHOTOS WERE FAKE. I'D NEED A VIDEO CAMERA. I WONDER WHAT THEY EAT . . . ?

"Green Hills of Faerie," said the bus driver, sounding bored. Danny reached up and pulled the cord.

The sound penetrated Christiana's reverie. She frowned. "Is this a cute name for a housing development or something?"

The bus stopped, and the kids filed off and into the world of fairies.

STRANGE NEW WORLD

"It's really . . . *green,*" said Wendell. Danny thought that was probably a bit of an understatement.

Faerie was ridiculously green. It looked almost absurdly lush. Rolling green hills ran to the horizon in every direction, except directly ahead, where a thick forest sprang up in even more shades of green. The grass was as thick as a carpet, spangled with violets and tiny orchids.

There were no buildings visible anywhere, just the road, which looped over a hill and out of

sight, and the bus stop. Come to think of it, the bus stop didn't look quite normal either . . .

"I think it's a tree," said Wendell, puzzled.

"Huh," said Christiana.

"C'mon," said Danny. He hadn't come to Faerie to stand around looking at bus stops. His mom needed rescuing! "I think that's the path over there. We're supposed to follow it, no matter what."

The path was also green, although it was a slightly different shade, and looked as if it had been mowed recently. A line of thin white pebbles ran along either side of it. Where it intersected the road, the pebbles seemed to be embedded in the asphalt, and the path picked up again on the other side.

"Which way do we go?" asked Wendell.

"Toward the forest," said Danny, shouldering his backpack. He wasn't sure how he knew, he just felt like his mother had to be somewhere in that direction. The others followed.

"Pretty place," said Christiana, after a few minutes. "I'm surprised it's not mobbed with people having a picnic or something."

The path ran down the hill, then up another hill, then down the other side. On the far side of that hill, there was a thin stream with stepping-stones across it. It was easy enough to cross, although Wendell cringed before
every jump, and stumbled
in the grass on the
far side.

Danny and Christiana looked at him. "What?" Wendell said. "I don't see all that well!"

"That's for sure, ye great oaf!" snapped a voice from the grass at his feet.

Wendell froze.

"Move, move!" said the voice. "Yer standin' on me wing!"

Wendell jumped backward, nearly landing in the stream again. From the grass, cursing bitterly, a tiny figure arose.

It was a lizard, about six inches high. He had the brilliant iridescent wings of a butterfly and the grim expression of a Mafia enforcer, and he was wearing a small red fez.

One wing was crumpled. The tiny lizard straightened it out, grumbling.

"You're a fairy!" said Danny, delighted.

THAT IS SO COOL!

"And yer a dragon," said the fairy, sounding less than pleased. "Nothin' but trouble, dragons. Always stirrin' things up and settin' things on fire . . . but at least you don't be steppin' on people!" He folded his arms and glared up at Wendell.

"Oh, jeez," said Wendell, crouching down to the fairy's eye level, or as close as he could get. "I'm really sorry. I didn't see you there. My depth perception . . ."

"*Depth perception,* is it?" The fairy spat on the ground. "Don't be using magic words at me, kiddo, or I'll be teaching you a few you won't like at all."

"This is seriously not happening," said Christiana to no one in particular.

"They're not magic words," said Wendell help-lessly. "They just mean I can't see very well. I'm sorry."

"Quiet!" Danny tried to shush her. "Don't make him mad . . ."

"What a trio," said the fairy, disgusted. "A blind klutz, a great fire-breathin' oaf, and . . . whatever you're supposed to be, kiddo." He transferred his glare to Christiana.

"Seriously, this is amazing." Christiana crouched down in front of the fairy. "If I didn't know better, I'd say it was real."

"Real!" Butterfly wings quivered in indignation. "And what do you be thinkin' I am, if not real?"

OH, C'MON. EVERYBODY KNOWS THERE'S NO SUCH THING AS FAIRIES . . .

"No such—no such thing—*NO SUCH THING!?*"

For being six inches tall, the fairy had quite a penetrating voice. After turning an alarming shade of puce with pure outrage, he stamped a tiny foot. Then, apparently feeling this was not quite enough, he tore his fez off and stomped savagely on it.

Christiana grinned broadly in appreciation. Wendell cringed.

The fairy leveled a shaking finger at Christiana. "For tellin' such a lie—and to me own face!—it's such a curse I'll be layin' on you! Thomas the Rhymer's curse, no less!"

"This is really amazing," said Christiana, looking around for the projector or puppeteer or whatever could be generating such a realistic image of a fairy. "They even got the grass tromped down and everything. I don't suppose it could be animatronic . . ."

Danny put a hand over his eyes.

The fairy stomped his left foot on the ground and muttered something, then stomped his right foot down and muttered something else. He caught up his tail, spun in a circle, then pointed at Christiana and narrowed his eyes.

Christiana looked suddenly startled and put a hand to her throat. "Whah-huh-hut?" she said, and broke into a coughing fit.

The fairy spun in another circle and drew in his breath to start again, when in a desperate attempt to be helpful, Wendell said, "You dropped your hat," and held out the battered fez.

The fairy stared at it, then let out a shriek like a wolverine with a toothache and snatched the hat from Wendell's hand. He yanked it down on his head, shot Wendell a look of pure loathing, and vanished in a puff of blue smoke.

"What did you *do*?" asked Danny, impressed.

I DON'T *KNOW!* I JUST GAVE HIM HIS HAT BACK!

THE CURSE

Christiana finished coughing, fished around in her backpack for a bottle of water and took a few sips.

"You okay?" asked Danny.

"I'm fine," she said. "That was weird . . ."

She stopped.

A very strange expression spread over her face, and her mouth worked for a moment, and then she said, all in a rush, "But it wasn't nearly so bad as I feared."

"Um," said Danny. "Okay. That's good . . . ?"

He started to turn back to Wendell.

 Danny had always suspected that Christiana was too tightly wound, and if one day, word went around the school that she'd finally lost her mind and been carted off to the Home for People Who Think Too Much, he would have been sad but not surprised. He hadn't expected her to lose her mind today, however, and he couldn't help but feel that it was a little inconsiderate, when he had a missing mother to worry about.

"Arrgh!" said the crested lizard, clutching her throat. "I didn't mean to say that last—it just came out, and really fast!"

"Is it just me," said Wendell, "or is she speaking in rhyme?"

Christiana pointed at Wendell and nodded furiously.

"The Rhymer's curse . . ." said Danny, fascinated. "Say something else!"

"It's got to be something psychosomatic," said Christiana darkly. "Because it feels like these rhymes are automatic."

It quickly became obvious that Christiana had to rhyme the ends of her sentences. If she tried to resist, she got red in the face and then sputtered out nonsense until she managed to come to a rhyme.

Danny thought this was hysterical. Christiana thought this was grounds for murder, something something something girder.

Wendell snapped his fingers. "I've got it! Try to say something that you *can't* rhyme."

Apparently trying to rhyme "orange" had given Christiana the mother of all coughing fits. She rolled around, tearing up handfuls of grass and hacking. Danny got out another bottle of water for her, and Wendell went digging through his book of fairy tales, looking for some kind of clue to her condition.

Eventually she stopped coughing. Her eyes were red and streaming. She took Danny's water grimly, muttered "Thanks, dude . . . I think I'm screwed . . ." and took a drink.

Under normal circumstances, Danny would have demanded that the Junior Skeptic try to explain away something so obviously magical as a fairy curse, but she looked so miserable that he felt a little guilty . . . and anyway, this wasn't getting them any closer to finding his mom.

"This is weird," said Wendell, flipping pages. "Thomas the Rhymer was a mortal bard—that's like a singer who tells stories—trapped in Faerie. He finally got loose, but they cursed him to tell only the truth, which made his stories pretty boring." He looked over at Christiana. "So she should be telling only the truth, not rhyming . . . Christiana, tell a lie."

She rolled her eyes. "I think Big Eddy's really cute. I want to kiss him on the snoot." Danny snickered.

"So obviously *that* isn't working," said Wendell.

"The fairy seemed pretty upset when you gave him his hat," said Danny. "Maybe you interrupted the spell and it settled on the rhyming bit."

"Yeah, about that . . ." Wendell turned to another page. "Some fairies vanish if you give them clothes, like brownies."

"Brownies?"

"Not the chocolate things. A type of fairy. They fix shoes. Maybe our fairy was one of those, and when I gave him his hat back . . ." The iguana shrugged.

"Well, if we run into any other mean fairies, throw your shirt at them," said Danny. He took a step down the path.

A shadow passed over them.

A *big* shadow.

Danny looked up to see something enormous pass over the sun.

EEEEP!

"That's a *big* bird," said Danny. "Wonder what it is." He looked over at Christiana—she always knew nerd stuff like that—and realized that during her coughing fit, she had rolled partway off the path. The line of white stones lay under her knees.

The shadow swept by again . . . and halted.

Stay on the path, Great-Grandfather Dragonbreath had said.

Danny flung himself at Christiana and grabbed her shoulder. "Wendell, help!"

Fortunately for Danny, Wendell's help was not required, because Wendell was still saying "What? Me?" when the bird struck.

It should have hit them. Six inches to the side, and it *would* have hit them. But the white stones seemed to act like force fields, and the bird missed. It scuffled savagely at the turf, then launched itself upward and was gone.

"Did you see the *size* of that thing?" asked Danny. "It had claws like—like—" He tried to think of a proper description and failed miserably. "Like really, really big claws!"

"The eloquence, it burns," said Wendell, picking himself up off the ground.

Danny straightened. "Well. I guess that's why we don't leave the path, huh? But we need to keep moving if we're gonna find Mom. Christiana, are you okay? I mean . . . err . . . with the rhyming thing?"

She stood up. "I'm sure that this will yield to willpower. I'll have it beat within the hour."

"Uh-huh."

"It should wear off at sunset," said Wendell. "Err . . . probably. Or else in a year and a day. Or seven years . . . I think those are the usual durations for curses."

...I DON'T KNOW WHY I'M TALKING IN VERSES.

"If all else fails, you could totally have a career in hip-hop," said Danny as they started down the path. Christiana gave him a look that was pure poison and muttered something under her breath. Danny wasn't quite sure what she'd said, but he was pretty sure it had rhymed.

OFF THE PATH

They reached the woods a few minutes later. The trees were tall, with silvery trunks and leaves that flashed golden when the breeze moved them. The air was full of rustling, and oddly colored birds sang from overhead.

The path stopped being grass and turned into springy green moss, but the white lines of pebbles continued under the trees. The kids kept walking, gazing up through the leaves.

"That bird has *horns,*" said Wendell, stopping suddenly.

Danny watched another bird go by that appeared to be made entirely of white lace. "This is pretty weird," he admitted.

"I think I've got it figured out, what this stuff is all about," said Christiana.

"Oh?" They kept walking.

Christiana folded her hands together. "We got too close to the mushrooms in your yard, and now we're hallucinating *hard*."

Danny and Wendell exchanged looks. "Well, if we wake up in the hospital, we'll know you're right," said Wendell philosophically. "And then we'll need kidney transplants."

"Really?" said Danny.

"There's a reason people don't eat toadstools. You know, the horrible death and all."

"That, or this is one of those dreams, and nothing's really as it seems," added Christiana.

"Go with that," said Danny. "Pretend this is a dream, and you have to help me find my mother before you wake up." He didn't really care *what*

Christiana thought was going on, as long as she didn't antagonize any more fairies.

Her face fell. "If this is a dream, it makes me sad . . ."

"Why?" asked Wendell.

"Means there's no flying monkeys to be had."

The iguana patted her shoulder. "You discovered a new species at summer camp. Finding another one on the weekend would be too much to ask." Christiana heaved a sigh.

The path led under a gnarled tree with low-hanging branches. A line of birds looked down at the travelers. They were all wearing small masks.

"That's not creepy or *anything*," muttered Wendell.

There was a rustling in the bushes a few feet from the path. Danny stopped. Wendell hid behind Christiana.

"Who's there?" asked Danny suspiciously.

"I can help you! Come over here!" a voice called back.

Danny took a step forward.

"I know what you're looking for!" said the voice in the bushes. "I can help you find it!"

The dragon started to take another step, and Wendell grabbed his shoulder. "Don't leave the path!" He pointed to the line of pebbles.

"It's just a few feet . . ." said the bushes coaxingly.

Danny wavered. He wasn't supposed to leave the path—Great-Grandfather Dragonbreath had been really clear about that—but it wasn't far, and if the voice in the bushes really could help them find his mother, wouldn't it be worth the risk? He lifted a foot.

Christiana stepped up to the line of pebbles and put her hands on her hips. "First tell us what we're looking for, or we're not taking one step more!"

Danny put his foot back down on the path.

"Stupid!" hissed the first bush. "Hardly anybody keeps sheep anymore. It's not like the old days!"

"It always used to be a lost sheep," said the second bush sullenly.

"Or babies," said a nearby rock. "Remember when we'd steal babies and leave changelings?"

"Man, those were the days," agreed the first bush.

Wendell nudged Danny in the ribs. "Fairies can disguise themselves as all kinds of things. I bet those aren't *really* bushes."

It occurred to Danny that his great-grandfather had been absolutely right—fairies were *not* nice.

"Out of curiosity," he said, "if I'd left the path, what would you have done to me?"

"Eaten you," said the rock.

"Made you dance until you dropped dead," said the second bush.

"Made you give up your hoard," said the first bush. "You're a dragon, right? We don't get that many dragons through here."

Danny snorted. His hoard was a fairly small collection, mostly bottle caps, coins from his allowance, and his birthday money, and he kept it stuffed in his mattress.

"Right. Better luck next time, guys." He turned his back and led the way down the path. The other two followed. Wendell kept a close eye on the rock.

STRANGE CREATURES

After the incident with the talking bushes, the kids went single file in the dead middle of the path. Probably things couldn't get them as long as they didn't break the line of white pebbles, but who wanted to risk it?

The forest grew stranger and stranger around them. Glossy green ferns grew taller than their heads, sending up curling fiddleheads nearly six feet high. Strange birds perched atop them. The most common wore small white masks, but there were birds with antenna and antlers and even one

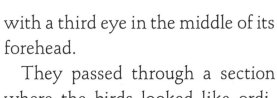

with a third eye in the middle of its forehead.

They passed through a section where the birds looked like ordinary blackbirds, but their calls were high, eerie giggles. It was incredibly creepy. Wendell put his hands over his ears and sang tunelessly just to try and drown it out.

"I'm all for species conservation, but maybe not in the case of this one."

"I know," said Danny, gritting his teeth as another chorus of giggling erupted from the trees. "I wish I had earplugs. Or headphones or something."

"Can you play an MP3 in Faerie? Seems like . . . err . . . something . . . dairy?"

The birds thought this was hysterical. Christiana sighed.

Eventually the giggling birds fell behind, and they were able to smack Wendell until he stopped singing.

A few minutes later, Danny stopped in his tracks.

There were miniature houses walking across the path in front of them. They were about four inches high and marching along on six small insect legs.

"Whoa," said Wendell.

No two houses looked alike. They were different colors and different styles of architecture. Danny picked up a tiny ranch house by the roof and flipped it over. It kicked its legs frantically. They appeared to be growing right out of the lower floor of the house.

"Now I know this is a dream, 'cause that's the weirdest thing I've ever seen," Christiana said.

The house slammed its front door in apparent agitation. "Sorry," said Danny, and set it back down on the moss. It scurried back into the line and continued marching across the path. After a succession of cabins, split-levels, and Tudors had passed, the final house—a trailer with a bent satellite dish—tromped past, and the path was empty.

Wendell looked at the line of house-bugs vanishing into the ferns, then at his book of fairy tales, and said, "Yeah, I got nothin'."

Danny shook himself. "Wow! Think what you could do with your own pet house! You could, like, teach it tricks, and keep stuff in it and take it to school as a lunch box . . ."

"I wonder if you can litterbox-train a house," said Wendell.

They kept walking.

The forest began to thin out. Shafts of sunlight stabbed through the trees. Birds flew through them, sometimes changing color when the light hit them.

"Look, there's something up ahead. I hope it doesn't make us dead," said Christiana, pointing.

TEARS OF A MAIDEN

Something lay half in, half out of the path. It looked like a pile of rags. It wasn't until they got quite close that they saw it was a fox lying in the ferns.

It didn't look good. It was so thin that each rib was visible, and its fur stuck out in ragged orange tufts. It lay on its side and watched them with bright, pain-glazed eyes.

"Careful . . ." said Wendell.

"There's something wrong with it," said Danny. He halted a few feet away and wrinkled his nose. Wendell waved a hand in front of his face.

Danny hadn't ever been that close to a real live fox before, and he hadn't realized that they *stank.* It smelled almost like a skunk—a sharp, burnt musk smell.

"I don't suppose you'd be willing to help a fellow out?" said the fox.

Wendell went "Yeeeerrk! It talks!" and jumped back, nearly into Christiana, who elbowed him sharply in the ribs.

"Help you how?" asked Danny. "And are you *really* a fox?"

"Vulpine's honor," said the fox, lifting a narrow black paw, "I'm truly a fox. A fox in a fix, in this case."

"Ah," said the fox. "Fairy curse, is it?" He squirmed along the ground an inch or two, but seemed unable to rise. "Happens around here. Should wear off once you're back in the mortal world . . . assuming you get back there at all."

"We're going back," said Danny. "We just have to rescue my mother first."

"Mmm." The fox gave another heave, and dragged himself a few more inches onto the path. "Might be able to help you, if you help me. Favor for a favor and all that."

"What sort of favor do you need?" asked Wendell warily. He felt bad for the fox, who was obviously having some kind of problem, but the memory of the murderous bushes was still fresh in the iguana's mind.

"There's a spell tangled in my tail," said the fox. "The thing that looks like a rope of thorns. It's weighing me down and keeping me from running free, as a fox rightly should. If you were to break it, I'd be very grateful."

"How do we break the spell?" asked Danny. He took a few steps closer and craned his neck. The fox had a long bushy tail, but sure enough, there was something wrapped around the end of it. It was hard to see quite what it was—it kept shifting oddly, and looked like purple thorns one minute and rusty barbed wire the next—but it definitely looked spiky and unfriendly.

"A few things will break a fairy spell without fail," said the fox cheerfully. "Cold iron, salt, holy water . . . don't suppose you brought any of those things?"

The children shook their heads.

PEELED ROWAN WAND BATHED IN FULL MOON'S LIGHT?

FRESH OUT.

NOT VERY WELL PREPARED, ARE YOU?

"We were kinda in a hurry," said Danny.

The fox sighed. "The tears of a maiden fair and true?"

There was a long pause.

"C'mon," said Danny, "it's the only way. And maybe he can help us!"

"No way, Jose!"

Wendell scuffed a toe in the dirt and muttered, "He looks like he's in pain."

"Indeed," said the fox pleasantly, "'tis quite excruciating."

Christiana sagged.

"Just a couple tears," said Danny. "Think of something sad! Think if my mom never comes back . . ." His eyes started to burn just thinking about it himself.

"I am not one of those people who cries on command!" snapped Christiana. She glared at Danny, Wendell, and the fox in turn, then stared up at the trees. "Not even if it's in demand!"

"But—"

"With a spell in my tail, I can't run," said the fox sadly. "And me with ten kits at home, starving, growing up fatherless if they grow up at all—"

"Oh, *please*." Christiana folded her arms. "All you've got at home are fleas."

The fox grinned, showing a thicket of sharp teeth. "Can't blame me for trying, fair maiden. Besides, I *might* have kits. Someday. Potentially."

Christiana grumbled something Danny couldn't make out, then something else that presumably rhymed with it.

"Look," said the fox, "I'm not unreasonable. I'll tell you what I know, and you can decide whether or not to help me. That's fair, isn't it?"

"Sounds fair," Wendell allowed. Danny nodded. After a minute Christiana did too.

"You're looking for someone," said the fox. "You said your mom might never come back, so I'm guessing she's been fairy-led, yes?"

"If you mean that fairies snatched her from a mushroom ring, yeah," said Danny.

The fox lifted his head as well as he could. The curse shimmered as it moved, and sparks crawled over it with a faint crackling noise. It looked very uncomfortable.

IF THE FAIRIES TOOK YOUR MOTHER, LIKELY THE KING HAS HER NOW.

THE KING OF THE FAIRIES?

INDEED, AND A NASTY CUSTOMER HE IS, MAKE NO MISTAKE.

"How can we get my mom back?" asked Danny.

"Mmm." The fox flicked his ears. "That's the question. The king likes flattery, so talk sweetly to him, but words alone won't do the trick. You'll have to trade him something he wants . . . one of your comrades, perhaps, or five years of your life, or the thing that stands behind the mill . . ."

"Not that one!" said Wendell, clutching his book of fairy tales close. "It happens all the time in the stories. Whenever anybody agrees to that, it turns out to be their daughter or something awful like that, who was standing behind the mill."

"I don't have a daughter," said Danny. "I'm a kid! And what mill? Like a windmill? You're going to have to slow down and translate for those of us that don't speak Fairy-tale Nerd."

Wendell gave him a withering look and went back to the book.

"He'd probably be willing to take your first-born," said the fox conversationally. "You know, when you *do* have one."

Danny didn't like any of these options. Five years of your life was a lot, and while Christiana could be annoying, he didn't feel right about trading her to the fairies for his mother. If he'd brought Big Eddy the school bully along, that would be a different story.

And while trading away his firstborn would be easy, Danny suspected that he might feel a little differently about it once he actually had kids.

"Possibly you can find something else to trade," said the fox. "I don't know. But it's best to go in being prepared." He wiggled a bit. "Now I've upheld my end of the bargain—will you uphold yours, maiden true?"

Christiana sighed and stepped up to the edge of the path. "You guys better hold my feet so I don't fall into the street."

There wasn't a street for miles around, but Danny and Wendell got the gist. Danny grabbed the back of her shirt, and Wendell grabbed her tail to keep her from rolling out of the path.

The coughing fit resulting from all those unrhymable words was truly impressive. For a minute Danny thought Christiana was going to have a seizure. She fell to her knees and nearly face-planted in the ferns outside the line of pebbles. Her shoulders shook, her scales rattled, and her eyes streamed tears.

Wendell dropped her tail, wiped his hand over her snout, and leaned out over the edge of the path, a single tear hanging from the tip of one claw. The fox trembled with excitement.

Christiana coughed harder. Danny was afraid he was going to have to sit on her to keep her from rolling off the path.

The tear fell onto the spell.

There was a shout that seemed to come from all directions of the woods, and the spell gave a great hiss and fizzle. The fox leaped to his feet, did a backflip, and tore off into the woods.

"That was awful," Christiana said, when the coughing finally stopped. She lay wheezing on the mossy ground. "Even worse than a whole-grain waffle."

"I don't know if I'd go that far," said Wendell, "but he could have at least said thank you."

"A fox's gratitude is like a fox's dinner," said a dry voice. "Both are soon over."

The trio whirled. Well, Danny and Wendell whirled, anyway—Christiana just groaned and put her arm over her eyes.

There was something standing by the edge of the path twenty feet away.

THE POWER OF THE SPOON

The creature looked like a cat . . . sort of. It was at least more like a cat than it was like anything else. It stood upright and had a long fluffy tail, enormous ears, and a hairless, gnarled face with sharp teeth.

It was black as char from head to toe, except for a white crescent on its chest.

It was also one of the ugliest things that Danny had ever seen.

"Err," said Danny. "Hi?"

It grinned. It had a lot of unpleasant-looking teeth. Danny went to school with a lot of kids who were very well-endowed in the dentistry department, so the sheer number didn't bother him, but the way they looked cracked and yellowed and broken certainly did.

"Hello, young masters," said the cat-thing, and bowed.

Danny looked at Wendell. Wendell looked at Danny.

"It can't get us if we're on the path," muttered Danny finally, and took several careful steps down the mossy road toward the monster. Wendell gulped and followed. Christiana sighed and plodded after.

When he was a little closer, Danny saw something that made his heart sink. The trees opened up into a sunny glade, and the ferns parted to reveal *another* path crossing theirs at right angles.

This one was also edged in white stones and was identical to theirs.

"Which way do we go?" whispered Wendell.

"I'm not sure," said Danny.

The cat-thing stood at the crossroads. It had black eyes with electric green pupils.

"Its eyes are weirding me out," hissed Wendell in Danny's ear.

Apparently the cat-thing had very good hearing. It grinned even wider and said, "We are as we were all made, are we not, young masters?"

Danny had met some really ugly things in his life, and they weren't all bad. The wrinkle-faced bat his cousin Stephen kept was kinda sweet, and the giant potato salad that lived in the sewers had been very helpful to him over the years.

Somehow he didn't think that was going to be the case with the cat-thing.

Still, if it had seen something that might help . . .

"You didn't happen to see my mom come by here, did you?" he asked. "Maybe last night."

The cat-thing's smile widened. "I might. I see many things with these eyes of mine." It glanced at Wendell. The iguana flushed.

"Well, did you see *that*?"

"That would be telling," said the cat.

"Um," said Wendell, looking into his book. "Are you a Cat Sidhe, by any chance?"

"It's pronounced *shee*," said the cat, "not *siddy*." The tip of its tail flicked. "And I am indeed." It eyed the book with dislike.

"What does the book say?" asked Danny.

"Not to trust it," said Wendell.

VILE SLANDER! I NEVER MET THAT BOOK IN MY LIFE.

"It says they like crossroads," said Wendell, turning the page. "And it'll try to lure us off the path."

"Lure is such an ugly word," murmured the cat. "Entice, perhaps . . ."

THEN IT'LL EAT US.

Danny looked at the Cat Sidhe. It gazed innocently up at the sky, lacing its claws under its chin. "Well . . . perhaps a nibble. A small one. Not so you'd notice . . ."

"Right," said Danny. "Never mind, then." He gazed at the three pathways. "I guess we just keep going straight and hope we catch up with my mom . . ."

"Wouldn't do that if I were you," said the Cat Sidhe, polishing its claws on the white splash of fur.

"So you did see them go by!" said Danny.

I MIGHT HAVE SEEN A LADY DRAGON GO BY, LAST NIGHT AT MOONSET. POSSIBLY.

"She was being fairy-led, you understand," said the cat.

"It's all in chapter two. Fairies use music to lead you places," said Wendell. "You can't help yourself."

"Actually, in this case it was a couple of guys with spears," said the cat. "But the same basic principle, I assure you."

Danny felt his blood boil.

THERE ARE FAIRIES POINTING SPEARS AT MY *MOM!?*

He advanced on the Cat Sidhe, feeling fire scalding the back of his throat. "Which way did they go? Tell me right now, or I'll—"

"Or you'll *what*?" asked the cat silkily.

"I'll—"

What exactly he might do—and Danny wasn't quite sure himself—was lost as Wendell grabbed his shoulder. The dragon tried to shrug the iguana off, but then Christiana was on his other side, hissing, "Do the math! Stay on the path!"

Danny looked down, and saw one foot hovering over the line of white pebbles.

The Cat Sidhe made a disappointed noise as Danny stepped back from the edge of the crossroads. His throat ached worse than the time he'd gotten strep, but getting eaten by some mutant fairy cat wasn't going to help his mom at all. Still, the fire had to go somewhere . . .

PTUI!

FWOOM!

OOPS.

WELL, THAT'S ONE FERN THAT WON'T MAKE ANY MORE TROUBLE . . .

"Very impressive, I must say. Pity nothing's real today."

Danny sighed. His anger was gone, replaced with weariness. He just couldn't win. Christiana finally got to see him breathe fire, and she was convinced that she was dreaming.

"Look," said Wendell, patting his shoulder, "we've been walking for hours. You've got, like, low blood sugar or something. Let's eat lunch. I know you put pudding cups in there."

Danny did not particularly feel like a pudding cup, but Wendell was probably right. Anyway, he had no idea which way they were supposed to go, so they might as well sit down here and eat.

The moss was soft and springy. The Cat Sidhe was still watching them intently, so the trio turned their backs to eat their sandwiches.

Danny picked at his peanut butter and jelly. Wendell, however, who was running on half a bran waffle from breakfast, devoured two and dug through his backpack for the promised pudding cup.

WHAT IS THAT?

Wendell paused with the spoon an inch from his lips.

"Ignore him," muttered Danny, "it's probably just another trick."

The Cat Sidhe let out a wail of despair, seemingly right over their heads. All three of them jumped, and Wendell threw himself flat, only to watch his pudding cup go flying.

Danny dove to keep Wendell from falling off the path—a pudding cup wasn't worth his friend's life, although given the bran waffle situation, he could understand if the iguana felt differently—but the Cat Sidhe was ignoring them completely. It was staring at the ground under its paws, growling softly to itself.

"Where is it? *Where did it go?*"

IS THIS WHAT YOU'RE AFTER, YOU UGLY MOOSE-PAFTER?

"Moose-pafter?" Danny whispered to Wendell.

The iguana shook his head. "Working with what she's got, I guess . . ."

The cat-thing, apparently untroubled by allegations of moose-paftering, said, "Yes, yes! That! What is it? Give it to me!"

It occurred to Danny that possibly his great-grandfather wasn't senile after all.

"Good gravy," said Wendell, while Danny's mouth hung open, "they really *do* have a thing about spoons!"

"Spoon!" moaned the Cat Sidhe. "Even the name is beautiful! O spoon, my spoon, by the light of the moon . . ."

"It's not *your* spoon until you dance to our tune."

Danny stepped up beside her. "That's right, kitty-cat! Tell us which way my mom and those guys with spears went, and then you can have the spoon."

The Cat Sidhe wrung its paws together. "Right," it said. "They went down the right path. Now give me the spoon!"

Danny took the spoon from Christiana and started to hold it out, but Wendell grabbed his arm. "Don't trust it!" the iguana hissed. "Make it promise!"

Wendell dug in his backpack, and quickly came

up with the sheet of notepaper he'd written the fairy oath on. "Promise you're telling us the truth," the iguana demanded, shoving his glasses up on his nose. "Swear by—um—'by ash and oak and rowan tree' that you're not lying."

The Cat Sidhe hissed like a boiling kettle and wrung its tail in its hands. "Nasty little lizards!"

"Look who's talking . . ." muttered Danny.

"They went left," said the cat angrily. "In the direction of the fairy king's court. By ash and oak and rowan tree, I vow 'tis true. Now give me the spoon!"

Danny looked at Wendell. Wendell nodded.

THEN GO GET IT!

The Cat Sidhe wailed and dove after it. They could hear the creature rooting through the undergrowth as they shouldered their packs and walked down the left-hand fork.

OR ELSE!

The path dipped gently downward, crossing a small brook and running in loops and zigzags through a weedy marsh. Strange plants grew from the boggy ground.

"That's a weird one," Danny said, pointing to a line of thick green tubes with spotted throats and oddly curled tops.

"Those are pitcher plants," said Wendell. "We've got them in our world too. They eat flies."

"Oooooh." Danny eyed the plants with new respect. "Wicked!"

"Mind you, the flies in our world don't usually wear hats . . ."

Danny was feeling better about life. Possibly it was the sandwich, possibly the knowledge that they were on the right track again. He was also very glad to learn that the fairies apparently really did like spoons, and that his great-granddad's oath seemed to bind them somehow. Things were looking up.

He continued to feel this way right up until they ran into the guys with spears.

The fairy guards were big, grown-up-sized reptiles, but they didn't look much like the lizard kids at school. They had large black eyes, and each one had an enormous set of wings, like a dragonfly's, coming out of his back.

They stood on either side of the path, and crossed their spears over it.

"Halt, travelers!" cried one. "Stand and be recognized!"

"Or else!" cried the other.

Wendell squeaked and hid behind Danny.

"Reptiles with insect wings? When will I stop seeing things . . . ?" asked Christiana.

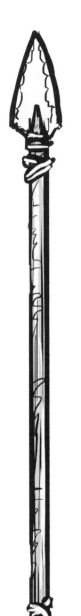

"Hmmmph!" said one guard. "A fool's errand, dragon-child. Go back to your home and your hoard."

"Or else!" said the other guard.

Danny took another step forward. He wondered if the guards could actually stab him if he was on the path. The spears were made out of some kind of stone, chipped into a leaf shape, and they looked awfully pointy.

"I'm going to see the fairy king," said Danny. "He took my mom, and I want her back!" He took another step forward.

"The king's court is not for the likes of you," said the first guard. "His Majesty does not welcome uninvited guests."

"Or else!" said the second guard.

There was a brief pause while everybody tried to figure out where that went in the conversation. The first guard sighed. "Morty, that's not when you say that."

"Oh. Sorry."

"He's my sister's kid," said the first guard apologetically. "He's not real bright, but my sister said I had to give him a job . . ."

"Or else!" said Morty happily.

Christiana put her hand over her mouth. Muffled giggles escaped through her fingers.

"Look," said Danny, putting his hands on his hips, "I'm going through, and I'm going to find the king and I'm going to get my mom back." He took a deep breath. He could feel fire in the back of his throat, where it had been burning ever since his mom had vanished into the fairy ring. "So you guys are gonna get out of my way . . ."

"Or else?"

"No, Morty, you don't say it when he's threatening us, you say it when *I'm* threatening *them* . . ."

Christiana put her face in her hands.

"We could go," said Wendell helpfully. "You know. Come back later when you've got your lines sorted out better?"

"Well . . ."

"If we see your sister, we'll be sure to tell her that you stopped us," added Danny.

"Oh, hey, would you?" The first guard looked pleased. "I'd appreciate that."

"Down this path, I assume?" asked Danny nonchalantly, stepping under the crossed spears.

"Most likely," said the guard. "You'll be sure to tell her that we stopped you?"

"In our tracks," said Wendell. "Thoroughly halted." The guard beamed as the trio sauntered away.

I CAN'T BELIEVE THAT WORKED . . .

Behind them, they heard the first guard saying, "Okay, Morty, let's go over this once more, and at least try to remember it this time . . ."

CAGED

The court of the fairy king lay in the middle of a clearing of ancient trees with gnarled trunks. The trees grew so closely together that the path had begun to run up the roots and partway along the fallen trunks, marked by chipped white lines of bark.

Long before they reached the clearing, they began to hear strange noises. First there was that high, haunting, desperate music that Danny had heard coming from the fairy ring—then it would break off, and there would be a skirl of whooping laughter, and deep grunting, slobbering noises, and the sound of distant voices.

A few hours ago, Danny would have found the noises creepy. After spending half a day walking through Faerie, they just seemed like more of the same.

The trio reached the edge of the clearing and looked inside.

Tall lizards with enormous dragonfly wings lounged about the clearing. They looked very relaxed. Some were eating and drinking. There were other, stranger things too—tiny creatures like puffs of dandelion down with big eyes, and lumpy, scabby creatures like bat-winged toads.

"Look, over there!" whispered Wendell by Danny's ear. "Under the big tree!"

In the center of the clearing was a tall oak tree, and under it was some kind of leafy pavilion. Vines grew over the pillars holding it up. A very tall lizard sat under it, with a pair of enormous white pigs on either side of him. Silver collars glittered around their throats.

"He's got pigs on a chain," whispered Danny. "That's pretty weird. I wonder if he's the king of the fairies."

"Not there," Wendell hissed. "Over *there!*"

He pointed. Danny followed the iguana's finger, and felt his stomach lurch.

"I don't want to cause you rage," Christiana whispered, "but isn't that your mom in that cage?"

Danny almost scorched his tongue and had to huff smoke out his nostrils. His *mom!* How dare they put her in a cage? Who did those fairies think they were?

Danny stormed into the clearing, not caring who saw him, planning to march up to the fairy king and demand his mom back *right this minute.*

He got about three steps out from under the trees, and an enormous watch-boar, which had been lying in the grass, rose up, grunting.

It was big. Really big. It looked about the size of a rhinoceros, and it had enormous tusks as long as Danny's arm.

"Danny!" Wendell, to his credit, ran *toward* the boar, although everything above his feet was trying to run *away* from it. "Danny, be careful! That thing is the size of a truck!"

"Pigs are really quite intelligent creatures," Christiana remarked to no one in particular. "Although manners aren't among their features . . ."

The boar let out a low warning squeal and stamped a hoof.

Danny drew in a breath to breathe fire. If it was really that intelligent, it had better not get between him and his mom.

"Tiddlywinks?" called a voice across the clearing. "Tiddly, what have you got?"

The boar dropped its head and pawed at the ground. Danny paused. It was one thing to breathe fire on a monster standing in your way— it was quite another to breathe fire on something named Tiddlywinks.

One of the butterfly-winged lizards flounced

up and surveyed the scene. "Oh, *toadstools,*" it said, annoyed. "Mortals in the Great Glade."

"You've got my mom!" said Danny. "And I want her back!"

YES, YES, VERY WELL, WHATEVER.

The lizard waved a hand. "I'm sure you have all kinds of demands. Mortals always do." It turned back to the giant boar.

Danny and Wendell waited. Christiana held out as long as she could, and then muttered, "Something, something . . . err . . . twitterpated."

"Fairy Valerian!" called a deep voice. "Are there intruders in the Great Glade?"

"Mortals, Your Highness!" said Fairy Valerian. It gave Tiddlywinks a last kiss on the snout and turned back to Danny and his friends. "You'd better go and see the king so that he can turn you into crawling worms and get it over with."

"I don't *want* to be a crawling worm . . ." said Wendell plaintively.

"Yes, well, you should have thought of that before you danced in the fairy ring or entered the ancient mound or walked widdershins around the standing stones or however you creatures keep sneaking in here," said Valerian. "Go on, shoo!"

DANNY VS. FAIRY KING

Danny and his friends approached the pavilion under the oak tree. Danny's tail lashed and his claws dug into the grass. Wendell was trying to hide behind his book of fairy tales. Christiana strolled along, watching the denizens of the glade with interest.

The fairy king was twice Danny's height. He had a shock of white mane around his face, and two long antennae rising from his eyebrows. His wings were dusty black, like the moths that flew around the porch light at night.

"What brings three mortals into my kingdom without my leave?" he growled, looming over Danny.

"You've stolen my mom!" cried Danny.

"It's possible," the king admitted. "I steal a lot of people."

"Yeah, well, that's her in the cage, right there!" Danny pointed.

At the sound of his voice, Danny's mom looked up. She grabbed the bars.

DANNY!

DON'T WORRY, MOM! I WON'T LET THEM KEEP YOU!

"Oh, her," said the fairy king. "Yes. She uprooted part of a fairy ring. I haven't decided her punishment yet. I'm rather leaning toward entreement. She would make quite a fine birch tree, don't you think?"

"You're not turning anybody into a tree!" Danny had no real idea how he was going to stop the king—was it hard to turn people into trees? Did it take a while? Did the spell stop if you got kicked in the shins by a dragon?—but before he could find out, Wendell grabbed his shoulder.

HEH. EXCUSE US JUST A MOMENT, O GREAT AND NOBLE KING . . .

He hauled Danny to one side. "You're doing this wrong!" he whispered. "The king likes flattery, remember? And we're supposed to trade him the spoons!"

Danny tried to get his temper under control. Wendell was right. If the fox was to be believed, the fairy king was powerful enough to turn them all into trees, or worms, or anything else he wanted. "Right," muttered the dragon. "Right. Okay. Yes. Flattery."

He took a few deep breaths and tried to squish the fire farther down in his chest. Behind him, he could hear Christiana say, "Marvelous oak tree you've got here, but I don't recognize the species, I fear . . ."

"Fairy oak," the king said. "They don't grow in your world. The acorns have to be buried by magic squirrels . . ."

DANNY!

His mom sounded frantic.

"Danny, don't trust him! He's not—"

"Danny, is it?" The fairy king waved a hand. Danny's mother's voice cut off abruptly. Her mouth kept moving, but no sound came out. When she realized she'd been muted, she grabbed the bars and shook furiously, but the wooden cage didn't budge an inch.

Danny turned back to Wendell and said, "I can't do this. I want to turn him into a giant s'more."

Wendell tore at his crest scales. "Okay," he said. "Okay. Just . . . just follow my lead."

Despite his rage, Danny was impressed. The iguana was always better at talking to teachers than he was, but Wendell was really laying it on thick. He hadn't known his friend had it in him.

"We have come across the breadth of your vast and marvelous kingdom to offer you a tribute, and to request a small boon in return, Your Highness."

"I like tributes," said the king. "Good tributes, anyway. But generally I like . . . oh, the firstborn sons of princes and footstools carved from the hooves of unicorns and so forth. What can you possibly offer me, lizard-child?"

Christiana stepped forward, opened her backpack, and pulled out a spoon.

"Ooooooooh. . . ." went the collective fairies.

The crested lizard displayed it to the crowd in the best game-show fashion.

"Aaaaahhhhh. . . ." said the crowd.

"For one so great, so magnificent, so . . . err . . . cool . . . as Your Highness," Wendell panted, starting to exhaust his store of flattery, "we have only the finest spoons of our world, suitable for, um, any occasion . . ."

The king leaned forward, fascinated.

Wendell licked his lips nervously. How much could you say about spoons? "The shiniest metal! The finest cutlery in the drawer! They're, um . . . the spooniest?"

"Surely, for such an awesome spoon Your Highness could grant us a little boon?" Christiana put in.

The fairy king stroked his chin, eyes riveted on the spoon. "What boon would that be?"

"Give us my mom back!" Danny shouted.

Wendell elbowed him. The fairy king's eyes narrowed. "Is the angry little dragon still here? I don't know . . . I was rather enjoying the prospect of turning her into a tree . . ."

Danny had no idea what he'd do if the king actually did turn her into a tree. Take her home and plant her in a nice pot in the backyard? Keep her watered with coffee? This was going to be hard to explain to his dad.

"Perhaps not for a single spoon, Your Highness," said Wendell smoothly, "but what about for this?" He reached into the backpack and came up with a fistful of silverware.

The assembled fairies rioted.

The king's eyes went wide, and he took a step forward. "All of those? For one mortal woman?"

"Do we have a deal, Your Highness?" asked Wendell.

It occurred to Danny where he'd heard that tone before. Wendell was *ruthless* at Monopoly. You generally heard that tone right before you discovered that you'd just handed over Broadway in exchange for Baltic and a couple of twenties.

"Give them to me," hissed the king, sounding not unlike the Cat Sidhe. He took another step forward and loomed over Wendell.

Wendell gulped. Danny jumped forward.

"Not until you promise!" the young dragon said. "Promise you'll let her go, and . . ." He turned to look at Wendell.

"Um," said Wendell.

"Where's the paper? Don't be a tapir!" hissed Christiana.

The iguana fished the sheet of paper out, looking sick to his stomach. "Uh-oh."

"What? What?" Danny leaned in. "Oh no!"

The paper was smeared with brown goop. Some of the words were still visible, but some had vanished, and others were blurred beyond recognition.

"Is that *pudding*?"

"It must have gotten on there when we were dealing with the Cat Sidhe," said Wendell wretchedly.

Danny took a deep breath. The king was tapping his foot impatiently.

OKAY. WE'LL HAVE TO IMPROVISE.

"We'll give you the spoons," said Danny, facing the fairy king, "all that we've got. And in return, you have to give my mother back, and swear by oak and ash and—um—" What was the third one?

"Rowan," put in Wendell.

"Right, that you won't turn her into a tree or try to stop us or do anything bad to us," said Danny.

"At all," Wendell added.

Danny wasn't sure that would be enough. He couldn't help but think that his great-grandfather's note had been a lot longer. "And, um . . . no funny business. And . . . err . . . no siccing giant birds on us. Or pigs. Or you'll get grounded!"

"Can you really ground the fairy king? That'd be . . . quite a thing . . ."

The king smoothed down his wings and said, "Agreed."

163

Christiana dumped out the spoons.

The king snapped his fingers. The cage opened, and Danny's mother rushed out.

"She's still mute!" said Danny, rounding on the king.

"You didn't ask about that," said the king, waving a spoon in his direction.

"We just gave you all those spoons!"

The fairy king grinned like a shark. "But what have you done for me lately, dragon-child Danny?"

Danny was ready to start burning fairy oaks down, but his mom grabbed his shoulder and tugged. When he turned to her, she jerked her head toward the woods and gave him a meaningful look.

"She's right. We should go," said Wendell. "Now, before he figures out something to do to us!"

They turned to run back to the path . . . and stopped.

A dozen identical paths led from the glade into the forest. Danny was sure they hadn't been there before.

Behind them, the fairy king started to laugh.

MEAN LITTLE CUSSES

"That's not fair!" Danny said.

"I'm not stopping you," said the king. "Go on. I wouldn't dream of *stopping* you." He examined his reflection in a spoon.

"Pick one," Wendell said desperately. "We have to hurry. I'm sure he's going to find a way to do something nasty."

Danny looked wildly between the paths. Where had they come in? There had to be a marker—something—

His eye fell on Tiddlywinks the boar.

"There!" said Danny, pointing. "That one! Come on!"

Kids and grown-up ran. The king made an annoyed sound behind them.

ALL THIS SUNSHINE IS SO BORING, DON'T YOU AGREE?

There was a roar of assent from his subjects. The king clapped his hands, and the sound seemed to roll through the trees, growing longer and louder and deeper, until Danny realized that it was thunder.

YOU SAID YOU WOULDN'T DO ANYTHING BAD TO US!

It occurred to Danny that when Great-Grandfather Dragonbreath had said fairies were mean little cusses, he had, if anything, been understating the case.

Thunder growled again. Rain began to slash at the leaves around them. The bright sky turned pewter gray.

"I don't like that guy," said Christiana, pounding down the path beside Wendell. "I think I'd like to see him fry."

Mrs. Dragonbreath, who generally believed in love and tolerance to one's fellow beings, gave Christiana an emphatic nod. She touched her throat and scowled.

"Is the muting stopping your breathing fire too?" asked Wendell, panting as he ran.

Mrs. Dragonbreath nodded.

Danny said a bad word under his breath. His mother tried to give him a stern look, then grinned ruefully and nodded.

They were skidding and slipping through the tree roots when suddenly the leaves started falling around them. At first Danny thought the rain was knocking them down, and then he realized that they were turning red and gold and brown, a whole autumn raining down in minutes.

"Seasons!" cried the voice of the fairy king in the distance. "I am tired of summer! Let us have fall and harvest and frost on the moon!"

The leaves did not so much fall as collapse. Wendell let out a squawk as a maple dropped its entire load directly on his head.

THIS ISN'T FUNNY!

Danny wasn't laughing. The leaf-fall had hidden more than Wendell.

"Where's the path?" asked Christiana. "We need to find—oh *bother*. Bath! Math! I can't find the path!"

"It's got to be here somewhere," said Danny.

It probably was there somewhere, but the sudden fall of leaves had covered white stones, white bark, and any other markers. They stood ankle deep in wet leaves, surrounded by bare trees, with the path completely hidden.

"We have to keep going," said Danny finally.

"But we'll leave the path!" said Wendell.

"It doesn't matter. If we stay here, it'll rain acid or bees or something and he'll claim it has nothing to do with us."

Danny's mom reached out and squeezed his hand. He looked up at her, wishing she could tell him what to do next, but she couldn't say anything, and even if she could, Danny doubted she knew any more about fairies than he did.

He took a step forward, and then another one. His mother wouldn't let go of his hand. When he looked back, she had taken Wendell's hand, and Wendell was grabbing hold of Christiana.

"Right," said Wendell nervously, putting his book of fairy tales back in his pack. "We should all hold hands. If we get off the path and get separated, I don't know how we'll find each other."

"Okay." Danny took a deep breath and plunged forward through the tree trunks. "Here goes nothin' . . ."

They'd made barely ten yards through the trees when Danny knew they were in trouble.

First there was a bird. It looked like a crow. It landed on a branch above them and croaked "Danny! Danny!" in a thick, raspy voice.

Figures staggered out of the woods, moving with jerky, shuddering steps. When they got a little closer, Danny realized that they were little more than sticks lashed together. They didn't have heads or hands or anything, just twigs animated by some malign magic.

The twig-creatures moved toward them, waving their arms. Wendell let out a yelp.

"Your name! Your great-grandfather said not to tell them our names, but he knows you're Danny—"

"Danny," agreed the crow.

"—and now the twig things are after you!"

Wooden claws closed on Danny's shoulder. Another one grabbed at his mother.

Despite their dire situation, Danny grinned.

Finally.

The fire that had been burning and roiling under his breastbone all day finally had someplace to go.

He spun on the twig-creature clutching at him and breathed fire.

It was a great flame. It was golden yellow and hardly any smoke came out of his nose. Even his dad would have been impressed.

The dry wood went up beautifully. The twig-creature dropped him and staggered back, flailing.

There were two twig-monsters trying to drag his mother into the woods. A touch of fire made them drop her immediately and run. Christiana succeeded in hauling Wendell free of the final twig-creature, and Danny sent it running.

The crow, seeing Danny turn in its direction, took off with a squawk.

"That's right!" yelled Danny after them, flaming wildly.

THA'TH'S—
RI'—WEH, CRU'TH . . .

WHAT'S WRONG?

I THIN'
I BU'NTH TH'
ROOTH UH MAH
MOUTH.

Wendell rolled his eyes. "Great. First you have to learn to breathe fire reliably, and then you have to learn to stop breathing it before you hurt yourself."

"If you're quite done burning Faerie down around our ears," said a familiar voice, "p'raps I might be of some assistance?"

They turned.

It took a moment for Danny to make out the speaker. Russet fur blended with russet leaves and made him briefly invisible. Then he grinned, showing white teeth, and Danny saw him.

"Come on," said the fox. "I can get you home, but you'll have to hurry."

HALT!

"Can you take us back to the path?" asked Wendell hopefully.

"The path is lost," said the fox. "You left it some way back, and once you leave it, finding it again is much harder. I can take you to the mushroom ring."

"That's how my mom got here," said Danny, nodding to his mother.

"Your servant, madam," said the fox, stretching his forelegs out in a bow. Mrs. Dragonbreath nodded politely.

"Can you fix her voice?" asked Danny.

FAIRY MAGIC RARELY SURVIVES A RETURN TO THE MORTAL REALM. NOW FOLLOW ME, AND QUICK!

They joined hands again, and followed the fox.

Their journey to the mushroom ring was a blur for Danny. The fox set a bruising pace and it was all the dragon could do to keep up with him. Leaves slipped and slid underfoot. Rain came down again, in a furious torrent, and then stopped. Mist rose from the ground, so that Danny could barely see the white tail-tip in front of him. There was even a brief flurry of snow.

He could hear Wendell whimpering and Christiana muttering furious rhymes behind him, but his mom's hand never left his.

Another twig-creature loomed up before them. Danny wasn't sure if he could breathe fire again so soon—his mouth was still sore—but it stumbled past them in the mist.

They broke out of the trees for a moment. Lightning stabbed a hilltop in the distance, and thunder snarled. They plunged back into the trees, and the fox pulled up short.

"Up ahead," he panted. "But the king thought of everything. There are guards."

"They're not allowed to stop us," said Wendell nervously.

"Do *they* know that?" asked the fox.

Danny let go of his mother's hand and crept forward, toward the mushroom ring.

There *were* guards. They looked nasty. They
had pigs. The pigs looked much nastier.

He gulped.

Mrs. Dragonbreath stepped up beside him and
gazed resolutely at the guards. She looked down
at Danny.

And nodded.

"Right," said Danny. "We can do this."

He stepped out of the trees and marched toward the fairy ring. The pigs looked up, grunting. They were as big as Tiddlywinks, and didn't seem nearly so pleasant.

"Halt!" cried one of the guards, brandishing his spear.

"No!" Danny yelled back. "*You* halt!"

"Oh, *that's* going to stop them. . . ." muttered Wendell.

Danny didn't care. The fairies might be twice as big as he was, the pigs might be the size of dump trucks, but it didn't matter. The fairy king had made a promise, and nothing was going to stop Danny from taking his mother through that fairy ring.

THE KING SWORE HE WOULDN'T STOP US! HE SWORE BY ASH AND OAK AND ROWAN!

The guard slowly lowered his spear. "He swore that?"

"Yes, he did!" called Wendell.

There was a long, long pause, while Danny thought it just might work.

And then the guard grinned a little—just a little—and his pig made a squeal that was almost a nasty little laugh, and the guard said, "Did he say anything about *me* stopping you?"

What happened next happened quickly.

Danny's mother lunged at the fairy guard. The fairy plainly hadn't been paying attention to her at all and went down under a hundred and sixty pounds of very angry female dragon. Christiana pounced on Wendell, shoved a hand into the iguana's backpack, and flung their very last spoon into the face of the nearest fairy. The fox leaped high in the air, right over the last fairy's head, and slapped him across the face with his brushy tail.

Suddenly there was no one at all between Danny and the fairy ring except one startled pig.

"Out of the way!" hissed Danny, staring at the pig. "Out of my way, or I swear by oak and ash and rowan that I'll turn you into *bacon!*"

Danny was never sure afterward if the magic words had been "ash and rowan" or "bacon," but the pig paused, and that gave Christiana time to yell, "The fairy king swore no pigs! Not even—um—um—ones wearing wigs!"

The pig looked deeply affronted at the notion that it might wear a wig, but it stepped grudgingly aside.

"Into the ring!" yelled the fox. "Quickly!"

"Go!" yelled Christiana, hauling Wendell forward. "Go, go, and don't be slow!"

Crested lizard and iguana half staggered, half fell forward into the ring of mushrooms. There was a flash of light, and they vanished before they hit the ground.

"Mom!" yelled Danny. "Mom, come on!"

Mrs. Dragonbreath rolled to her feet. She was carrying the fairy's spear. The fairy was lying on the ground, curled into a little ball, and did not seem interested in getting up any time soon.

Danny reached out and grabbed her hand.

HOME, SPOONLESS HOME

"Well," said Danny's mother. "That was . . . something."

All four of them lay in the garden. The mushroom ring had mostly been crushed by their passage. Danny sat up and felt fungus squish under his knees.

"I don't think we'll be going through that ring again," he said. And then something else occurred to him. "Mom! You can talk!"

She put a hand on her mouth. "So I can. Thank goodness!"

Wendell let out a bleat of disgust. There was mushroom goop all over his shirt and hands. He tried frantically to scrape it off his fingers, but since both hands were covered, all he did was transfer it from one hand to the other.

GET IT OFF,
GET IT OFF!

BLECH!

I HAVE NO IDEA WHAT JUST HAPPENED, BUT I THINK I JUST HAD A REALLY WEIRD DREAM. POSSIBLY I'M *STILL* HAVING A WEIRD DREAM. I'M NOT SURE.

Christiana put down the hose and glanced around at the other three. "And you were there, and you were there . . . also there was something about pigs and spoons."

"Definitely a dream," said Danny hurriedly. "We, uh, were hanging out in the backyard, and you fell asleep. You've been out for hours."

Wendell gave him a look.

"It's just easier this way," muttered Danny. His mom hurriedly shoved the fairy spear in with the rakes against the side of the house.

"Ri-i-ight," said Christiana, giving them a suspicious look. "Asleep. *Really.*"

"Do you have a more logical explanation?" asked Wendell, looking innocent.

. . . No.

"You were asleep out in the sun," said Danny helpfully. "Maybe you got, like, sunstroke or something. I hear that gives you totally weird dreams."

The look Christiana gave them indicated that she was not particularly convinced, but she only said, "I should get home before Dad starts to worry." She shouldered her backpack and headed toward the gate in the fence.

"I think your girlfriend's ticked off," said Danny, not quite under his breath.

"We're just lab partners," said Wendell, with dignity. "And I should get home too. I'm supposed to be doing chores." His stomach growled. "And

I could really use a snack. All that time in Faerie, and nobody offered us fairy food or anything. It's supposed to be awesome, except for the bit where you can't ever leave." He paused at the gate. "Glad you're back. Mrs. D."

"Me too, Wendell. Thanks." She leaned down and kissed the top of the iguana's head. Wendell flushed and ducked out the gate.

"Well," said Danny, when they were both gone. "I guess that's that. Typical morning. Go to Faerie, save world, all in a day's work."

Danny couldn't believe the injustice of it all. He'd rescued his mother from the evil clutches of the fairy king, faced down Cat Sidhe and twig-creatures and giant pigs, and she was *grounding* him?

"Do you know how dangerous that was?!" his mom yelled, throwing her hands in the air. "You could have been killed! He could have turned you all into worms!"

"He was going to turn you into a *tree!*"

"All right," said his mother, finally. "As long as you swear never to do anything like that again—ever—under *any* circumstances—"

"I'd totally do it again," said Danny. "You're my *mom!*"

"Oh Danny . . ."

She hugged him. Danny glanced around to make sure that Wendell had really gone before hugging back.

"Fine," she said, sighing. "You're not grounded." She stomped into the house. Danny found her drinking cold coffee directly out of the coffee-pot. "I'll get a rototiller in tomorrow and get out the last of those mushrooms. And I'll call Grandfather and let him know I'm not dead." She sat down at the kitchen table next to Danny and put her chin on her hand. "I suppose there's only one thing left to do . . ."

"What's that?"

"Figure out how we're going to explain to your father that there are no spoons left in the house . . ."

HAVING BAD DREAMS? CALL DANNY DRAGONBREATH!

DANNY DRAGONDREAMBUSTER AT YOUR SERVICE.

DANNY DRAGONBREATH's best friend, Wendell, has been having some awful dreams lately . . . full of horrible bran waffles his mom is forcing on him, impossible pop quizzes, and monsters. But these are no ordinary nightmares . . . and Wendell might just go permanently insane if Danny and Wendell's *not*-girlfriend Suki don't delve into his dreams and save him.

BUT WHAT ELSE MIGHT THEY DISCOVER IN WENDELL'S STRANGE AND NERDY BRAIN?

EEP.

FIND OUT IN THE EIGHTH BOOK IN THE DRAGONBREATH SERIES:

NIGHTMARE OF THE IGUANA
COMING SOON!